Lik opyri) Pirnie Primary Sch ҁ)15
Libr Firs ublishea Great Britain

WhiteWater Publishing Ltd

ISBN 978-1-909797-32-1

A catalogue record for this book is available from the British Library

INTRODUCTION

Everyone at the Festival Theatre is delighted to have been able to work with Craigroyston, Forthview, Pirniehall and St David's Primary schools over the past two years bringing all their Primary 6 and Primary 7 pupils to the theatre several times, and then supporting their creative work in schools by providing artist led workshops.

The young people have experienced Dance, Music, Puppet-making and creative writing. They have made their own work inspired by their visits to see live performances and have exhibited their work.

Following a visit to see the National Theatre's production of 'The Curious Incident of the Dog in the Night-Time' all of the Primary 6 and Primary 7 pupils at the four schools worked with author Nick Thorpe and poet Elspeth Murray who inspired the pupils to write their own Curious Stories.

This volume of fantastic stories is the result.

The Festival Theatre will be working with the four schools for one more year and they will see more shows and experience more artist led workshops. We hope the young people will continue to come to live performances long after our intervention is over, and for the rest of their lives.

The Festival Theatre would like to thank the pupils for their hard work and their teachers for supporting them throughout the production of their creative work and for organising their trips to the theatre.

Cerin Richardson, Learning & Participation Manager

COMMENTS FROM
PIRNIEHALL PRIMARY SCHOOL

"We all had a fantastic time during the workshop. The children were fully engaged throughout and were very excited about getting their ideas down on paper. They used the suggestions given to them at the workshop while they were writing these stories.

We have never seen the children so enthusiastic about story-writing!

This has been a great experience for everyone!

We would like to say a great big thank-you to Mrs Forsyth and Miss Paterson for all their help and support during the writing process and to Nick Thorpe and Elspeth Murray for their input during the workshop.

Also a huge thanks to the Festival Theatre involving us in their fabulous events! "

The Staff at Pirniehall Primary School

AUTHORS

JANET MCEWAN	DECLAN CUMMINGS	JACK BROWN
SARAH MICHELE WILSON	LUKE FOXTON	LUCY MCDONALD
AMY DIANE MCDONALD	SINEAD BOYLE	KAI DALGLEISH
DERIN HUNTLY	EVE MACLEOD	BEN WANLESS
JORDAN NYE	DECLAN MCLEAN	REECE LOTHIAN
AARON MACINTOSH	TAYLOR RAMSAY	SHAHED METGAWIL
DYLAN MACINTOSH	AARON DICKSON	CALUM TAIT
DYLAN WHALEN	MIA KUTLUOL	MARCIN
MARWA AL DEAN SALEEM	KEVIN KERNACHAN	STRZESZNIEWSKI
HASSAN AL-SAYAFI	DILLON HANNAH	JACK ANDERSON
JACOB GAJOSZ	BLAKE GIBSON	CLOE LYONS
JODIE SIMPSON	THOMAS HUGHES	ANGEL PRESTON
LOGAN SMITH	VICTORIA BLACHOWICZ	LEWIS HUNTER
ERRYN PITTS	ADAMA KRUBALLY	JASON BATEMAN
NADA AMSAAD	BROOKE CLAPPERTON	KAL BRECHIN
PHOENIX BROWN	ELLIE LOGAN	LANA WILSON
REHAAN SUBHANI	FRANK LOW	REBECCA WILLIAMSON
BEN DEVRIES	ELLIOT DEVRIES	GEORGIA GARDINER
SAFA AL-DEAN SALEEM	SEAN MCCORMACK	CAITLIN BRECHIN
LEWIS MARSHALL	LANA WILSON	JACK MACLEOD

CONTENTS

MR MOONSTONE BY JANET MCEWAN (P6)

One day Mr Moonstone was watching the news. There was a swimming competition to swim to China. Mr Moonstone loved the sound of that and his family were in China but there was one problem... Mr Moonstone can't swim! So he decided to make a boat.

First, he gathered wood. Then he collected sticks. Then he made a diagram of the boat. Finally, he started making the boat.

Two months later, the boat was eventually finished. So, Mr Moonstone set off to sea. He was very bored while he was at sea for 49 days. One day, Mr Moonstone saw land. He jumped out the boat and swam to the land. As soon as he got there, he saw someone that looked very similar to himself. They looked at each other. The boy ran over hugging Mr Moonstone. "You have won the race!" said the boy. Mr Moonstone had forgotten about all about the competition to swim to China.

The boy handed him a medal saying well done. Shaking his hand, Mr Moonstone asked him his name.

The boy replied "My name is Sir Moonstone. You ARE MY BROTHER!"

"Fantastic" said Mr Moonstone. He felt so excited, he had a long lost brother!

Sir Moonstone showed him around. Mr Moonstone bought a house in China and they lived happily ever after.

LILY, THE MISSING BABY FOX
BY SARAH MICHELE WILSON (P6)

When I got up this morning, my baby fox, Lily was gone. I wonder where she is? I decided to go and hunt for her. But I must call Lily's brother Tylor and her dad John. Calling Tylor… "Hi mum what's up" said Tylor. "Oh it's your sister, I can't find her", I said. "Yeah I saw her earlier she said she couldn't wake you up this morning because she was a bit hungry", Tyler said.

"What way was she going?" I said.

"Right no left no! I can't remember, sorry mum, right I have to go now, see you soon, I hope you find Lilly", said Tylor.

"Bye mum, bye",

"Bye sweetheart", I said.

"Honey, I'm home" said John.

"Oh have you seen Lilly? She's gone!" I said.

"No I haven't, why?"

"I can't find her anywhere!" I said.

"I'll go look for her", said John.

"Mummy, it's Lilly! Mum I'm on a boat. I thought I saw you! I'm going to jump off this boat before it goes somewhere. Here I go - jump! I'm off… Right where am I? Mum, Dad. Where am I? Can you hear me? Can you see me? Come on tell me! Please!

"Lilly I can hear you" said John.

"Daddy!" said Lilly.

"Stay where you are. I see you. Come home Lilly", said John.

"No, I'm not coming because mum didn't wake up this morning and I was hungry!"

"Well I'll make sure she'll be up tomorrow ok, or I'll get you up with food", said John.

"Ok, Daddy lets go see Mummy"

THE STATUE IS ALIVE BY AMY DIANE MCDONALD (P6)

3:AM

The cleaners came in to Alex's bedroom and spilt some strange medicine on the statue in Alex's room. Then the cleaner left the room but the statue moved just a little bit. 10 minutes later, Alex ran in to his room and he said "What is going on?"

6:AM

"Oh my God, the statue is alive but how? What happened during the night mum? Mum! The statue is moving!

Alex's mum said "No it is not stop telling lies Alex".

"I am not!"

"Let me see". The statue moved back in to place when Alex's mum opened the door. He thought it was magic but was suspicious on how his mum just opened the door and the statue moved back in to place. He sneaked out to the old science building.

9:AM

Friday night Alex found a key to get in to the science building. He opened the door of a cupboard and found a bottle with my mum's name on it.

So, it must be Alex's mum, or has the statue been alive all his life...?

DRAGON ATTACK BY DERIN HUNTLY (P6)

Once upon a time, there were two brothers. They were best friends. Then, an earthquake happened and left a massive hole in the centre of the earth. George had fallen into the green slime and was hanging on to the edge of the hole by his fingertips. James looked down the hole and he heard the roar of a dragon coming out of the darkness. "Get back brother"! Screamed George. "I thought you fell in the hole"? Asked James. George explained that he had used his strength to climb back out. "We need to find something to kill the dragon with", he said. James agreed and together they got shovels, dug under the military bunkers into the plasma rocket room, took one rocket and walked back towards the city and the dragon. On their way back, they encountered the terrifying beast with its sharp teeth like knives. They hid behind a car. Then, they aimed the plasma rocket at the dragon. The dragon shot a fire beam but the beast missed his target. It looked shocked that he had missed. Then, George and James aimed with the plasma rocket and shot the dragon in the chest and broke the dragon's heart. The dragon was finally dead!

James and George became heroes and grew up to become dragon slayers.

DETECTIVE BIRD BY JORDAN NYE (P6)

Arthur woke up and stretched his wings then looked at the ground. Then he saw his owner, Jeff, and blood on the floor. He wasn't sure if he was unconscious or dead. In his head he said," I need to find out who killed Jeff! Oh, wait! I'm locked in my cage! If only that dog could help me – SQUALK!"

In came the dog. It put the key in its mouth and opened my cage. Arthur said "Thanks mate!" in his head and walked away. The adventure awaits.

"I know I'll become a detective!" said Arthur. "SQUALK! Dog, did you see the person that did this?" "Yes, I think I did!" said Dog. "Where did he go?" asked Arthur. "To the airport – he went to France!" exclaimed Dog.

So they went to France...

The suspect was at the top of the Eiffel Tower. It was a parrot too! But Arthur couldn't fly so how could he get up there? He climbed the flagpole and jumped across – he made it! Dog took the stairs. Arthur came face to face with the suspect! Dog crawled his way to the top of the tower. "I see you've found the killer then" puffed Dog. "You killed Jeff?!" asked Arthur, astonished. Dylan the parrot replied "YES!" and laughed loudly. "Why?!" cried Arthur. "Jeff killed both my parents! I loved them and I had to avenge their deaths!!" wailed Dylan.

I wonder why Jeff killed Dylan's parents? But that's another story...

DRAGON DREAMS BY AARON MACINTOSH (P6)

Once there was a boy called Bob. He was walking down the hill, happily eating crisps.

He saw his friend Jimmy on the bench talking to his self.

"Jimmy" Bob said quietly "Jimmy, are you ok ?"

"Yes " said Jimmy

"Let's go home " said Bob

"Yes we better go now " said Jimmy

They went home and then they went to bed .Bob had a dream. He went in the forest. He saw a DRAGON. Then he saw Jimmy .Bob went over to Jimmy and said, "Look that's a dragon, a black one with blue eyes. Look its going down. Let's go and see it"

"OK" said Bob "but I am….."

"Just do it .OK " interrupted Jimmy

"We are here " said Bob. "Look at that. It's a fish! Let's give it to the dragon "

"OK" said Jimmy

The dragon ate the fish and they became friends. The boys saw a saddle and put it on him. Bob and Jimmy had a ride on the dragon. They went flying over the trees.

"This is cool ", said Bob

Just then Bob woke up and said "Jimmy, Jimmy I just had an awesome dream!!

THE MAGIC BASKET BY DYLAN MACINTOSH (P6)

One day there was three boys called Bob, Jimmy and Dylan. They went to the shop and bought a magic basket and went to a food shop and bought apple juice, a sandwich and some crisps. They went to the beach and got changed into swimming stuff and put the basket down so they could go into the sea. The basket ran away!!

They chased the basket and they ran after it but it got away so they went to the chip shop and got fish and chips instead. They went to Bob's house for a sleepover and watched a movie called Fast and Furious Seven. After the film they went to sleep. In the morning they went to play football in the park.

MAX AND THE BEAR BY DYLAN WHALEN (P6)

The bear lived in the zoo. The bear was brown and it was a male.

Max felt very happy when he saw the bear. He was also happy because he got to feed the bear. Max was the zookeeper. Next day Max went to the zoo and it was a sunny day. Max took ice-cream to the bear and the bear liked it.

Max tried to take the bear home with him but he couldn't get it in the car! So he tied a pair of roller skates onto the bear's feet and then Max began to push the bear along the street!

After ten minutes of pushing, a police car pulled up next to Max. "What are you doing?" asked the policeman. "I'm taking the bear home," explained Max. "Oh no you're not!! Get him back to the zoo RIGHT NOW!!!" shouted the policeman.

Max took the bear back to the zoo. Max doesn't work at the zoo any more – but he still goes to visit the bear and give it ice-cream.

THE EGG HUNT BY MARWA AL DEAN SALEEM (P6)

One day, I woke up and my mum came into my room with pots and pans banging them together. Mum shouted "Wake up sleepy head!" "Why mum?" I replied. "Because we are going on an egg hunt" said mum.

10 minutes later, I have found 24 eggs! I ask mum if I can eat the chocolate eggs and she says yes. I start to munch on the first one when the egg in my hand starts moving. Why is it moving? The egg cracks. It is green and gooey inside. An alien comes out!

I show my family what has happened. Dad says he has a friend with a rocket that we can put the alien in. Let's send it back to space!

10 seconds to go...10,9,8,7,6,5,4,3,2,1.

BLAST OFF!

TOM AND THE ALIENS BY HASSAN AL-SAYAFI (P6)

Once Tom was in his first day at his new school. He made a friend called max and Jordon and max show Tom all the school and class.

"It home time Tom" said max, "do you want to come with me?"

"Yes" said Tom, "do you want to go to the park?"

On the next day Tom went to the school suddenly Tom stop he never herd any noise in the school Tom went in the school where is everyone max why are you here because the aliens have taking all the school.

OCEAN ADVENTURE BY JACOB GAJOSZ (P6)

David had a dream about the ocean. He dreamt he had found treasure.

The next day, David decided to go to the ocean and search for pirate gold. He said to himself, "this is impossible"!

David then found a boat.

He made a plan and picked up food, water and a harpoon from home.

The next day, David went back to the ocean with his supplies. He jumped in the water and a shark attacked him. David picked up his harpoon and killed the shark but in the fight, he broke his boat and forgot about the gold. Oh no!

David wasn't going to give up. He went back again the next day and had a very lucky day because his eyes spotted the gold in a pirate box at the bottom of the ocean! There were old pictures and $1000 inside. It was a good day for David.

David used the money to buy a new boat.

David is no longer scared of sharks!

THE WOLF THAT RAN AWAY BY JODIE SIMPSON (P6)

There was a boy called John. John had 2 pet wolves and he fed them once a day. But one day, John was wearing a brown top while he was feeding the wolves. When John turned around to put the food down, one of the wolves ran away from John. But John didn't know why. He was very sad because one of his wolves had ran away. John ran after the wolf. He chased the wolf into town. John was so worried about his wolf because of the traffic that he managed to rip his brown top on the way.

The police noticed John's torn jumper and stopped him. "Where are you going"? Said the policeman. "I need to find my pet wolf", said John. But the police laughed at him. John felt like he was going to cry. He went to a shop to get a new jumper so he was not cold. John picked a brand new, green jumper and put it on. He then went to the bus stop to see if he could find his wolf. John found the wolf sitting waiting for the bus to go home. The wolf leapt on him and couldn't wait to go home! So John realised "my wolf had ran away because I have a brown top on"!

CHASED BY MUTATED FOOD BY LOGAN SMITH (P6)

One day, I was strolling home from school.

Then, boom! Some apples, grapes, oranges and crisp packets even a couple of sweet wrappers appeared.

I was thinking to myself, "What the heck is going on?"

Then, I heard some annoying rustling noise so I turned around.

They started to grow arms and legs!

Then they started going after me, and then I did a runner.

I bolted as quickly as I possibly could without getting caught.

I thought it was a weird occurrence.

As a matter of fact, it never happened until now.

I think I`m tripping out of my head.

It`s weird.

I don't know why but I think it`s a dream.

Then I woke up and realised it was just a dream.

LOST IN THE WOODS BY ERRYN PITTS (P6)

One day, Claire and Ruby were going to school camp. They asked each other to be each other's partner. Miss Bossy told the class to line up so they did. Claire and Ruby were excited. They got on the mini bus and it took 2 hours to get there. Miss Bossy told everyone where they were sleeping. Claire and Ruby were in the same room. The teacher called everyone back and said that they were going on a little walk. Claire and Ruby went back to get their rucksacks. It had been half an hour since they left. "I want to sit down!" moaned Ruby. "Ok" said Claire, fed-up. So they sat down and had a little chat but when they were talking they did not see the class walk away!

Ruby jumped up and said "WHERE ARE THE CLASS?!!! THEY HAVE GONE!!! Ooh no! We have to find our class!" "Ok! Ok! Ok! Right, we need to start making shelter" said Claire. Ruby saw two trees. "Aaaaah!" she said "We can use them!" An hour later, they finished making their shelter for the night. Ruby looked in her rucksack and she had sleeping bags and together they had four apples. They went to sleep frightened and cold. The next day, Ruby and Claire got up and started looking for the class but Claire heard a noise and said "That must be our camp!" So the girls sprinted back to the camp and no-one even noticed they had been gone so the girls got changed and started to play with their other friends.

THE LOST JOURNEY BY NADA AMSAAD (P6)

Once upon a time, there was a boy and a girl named Emma and Jack. They were siblings and they were both 12 years old. They went on holiday with their parents but one day when they all went shopping, Emma and Jack lost their parents.

Emma was crying. Jack said "don't worry, we'll find them". They looked all over town and they couldn't find them anywhere. They were very sad. They decided to go back to the hotel and sleep in their holiday tree house. Neither of them slept very well.

After their long night in the tree house, they woke up and Jack said "we need to go back home". "What? Why?" said Emma. "Because we have to, now stop asking questions and lets go" said Jack. They were on the plane for seven hours back home to Miami, USA. When they got off the plane, they heard someone crying. They turned around to find their parents standing there. Emma and Jack ran over and gave them a massive hug. Jack asked his Mum "where have you been"?

"We have just come off that plane! Where on earth have you two been?" said their Mum.

"We have been on that plane as well" cried Emma.

"No way" said their Dad. "How funny is that, let's go home anyway"! They all went home happy.

MOTION MOVER SAVES THE DAY!
BY PHOENIX BROWN (P6)

One day, a boy called Conner joined a football team. On Sunday, he had his first game, he was so happy about it. Conner got the ball but someone got it off him... oh no they scored! But it was not over yet. Conner's friend scored just before half time. The team all got a drink of water and of they go again. There was something not right at all. All of Conner's team were just standing there. Conner went to the other team and said "why are they like that"? Jamie, the other team Captain said, "I'm not too sure".

Conner was worried and started thinking out loud, "I need to try and make friends with Jamie and work out what we can do". Jamie replied, "Yes I'll help you. Nobody knows what happened"

" Maybe they just don't want to play"? Said Jamie.

" It could be the water", replied Conner.

"Ok, let's call the water people", said Jamie.

"Hi! I think you guys have done something to the water" said Jamie on the phone to the water people.

"Oh no! I think I have given you guys the water with something in it that was meant for someone else! It makes people freeze for up to 5 hours" said the water company.

"What will we do now"? Said Conner, worried and confused.

Jamie remembered a drink called 'Motion Mover'.

"Let's make them drink it. Then it will take 1 hour and they will be much better"!

So that's what they did. The boys went on to win the football game and nobody drank from the water bottles again!

A CRISP PACKET FOLLOWS ME HOME
BY REHAAN SUBHANI (P6)

I was walking from school I heard a rattle I turned around it was a Walkers crisp packet so I carried on waking. I looked again - it got closer so I ran!

It chased me all the way home. I stopped at the traffic lights and it kicked me so I kicked it and it went flying. I walked home. I shut the door. I heard a knock so I opened the door...

It was the Walkers crisp packet!

It was evil!

I got a cage from the cupboard and tried put it in but it managed to escape. I looked round the house but couldn't find it! Later that night it attacked me when I was sleeping...

I was lucky I had a pocket knife in my drawer. I split it in half and I threw it out the window. It landed on a really hot engine and melted but it still got up and ran for me. I shut all the windows and doors and holes and cracks.

It tried to come in but it got run over by a lawnmower! I was so happy! But when I told my best friend Aaron about it, he didn't even believe me!!

THE ALIEN TEST BY BEN DEVRIES (P6)

Logan Smith was lying in bed, happy and content when his mum scared him with a scream so loud that it made his dad go deaf in one of his ears!

Dad sprinted up the stairs, shouting "What is going on"? Then Logan said that mum had been poisoned by someone! Dad told Logan he had to go to bed so that Dad could think about what to do.

When Logan woke up in the morning to go to school, he realised that Dad wasn't there... Where has he gone?

Logan waited all day for Dad to come back but then he heard a noise outside his front door. There was a note outside the door. It said…

"Logan if you want your dad back , you need to come to our spaceship so that we can test how intelligent the human brain is".

The aliens took Logan to space so that they could test him on how smart he was. He scored an A plus and all the aliens were surprised how smart an earth boy could be. They released dad from their space jail and together, Logan and Dad went home.

THE AMAZING DANCERS BY SAFA AL-DEAN SALEEM (P6)

Dunyah was laughing excitedly because she had come 1st place in her solo dancing competition. Safa, her big sister had also come first place in the U12 competition. Safa and Dunyah counted the trophies that they had won. There were 12 trophies altogether.

Dunyah and Safa's mum couldn't believe it!

She said, "You will become a champ by the end of this year"!

But Safa and Dunyah disagreed. They both replied, "We'll become champions by the end of the next competition"!

Their dance boss is called Derek he said, "There is a competition at Meadow Bank and there is a solo and slow pairs category."

Safa and Dunyah danced in the solo category where they both came in 4th place. Safa and Dunyah both came 1st place in the solo category. Their mum was happy as it was Dunyah's first competition and championship. When they got home all of their sisters were so proud of them including Safa and Dunyah's big sister Deanah.

Safa and Dunyah were laughing because they had become a champion, not even just a champion but a prom champion. *YAEHYEAHYAEH!*

THE BEARDED DRAGONS BY LEWIS MARSHALL (P6)

Jimmy has a dream. He dreams that when he wakes up he will be on an island. Not just any island. An island where there are loads of new born, bearded dragons. It takes 100 miles to get there because the only way to travel is by boat. When he gets off the boat, he grabs the massive, dragon catching cage and he heads to the middle of the island. Jimmy hears a noise. He turns around and sees ... a Komodo dragon! Jimmy ran to find shelter and safety.

The next morning, Jimmy wakes up to a frog jumping on his face. He flicks the frog away and starts to make breakfast. The only thing he has to eat is fish. Jimmy heads for a swim and after he gets dry, he starts to hunt for new born, bearded dragons.

All of a sudden, Jimmy hears splashing. He turns around and there are two water walking dragons playing in the sea. He catches them with a large net and puts the new born bearded dragons in the massive cage with some food and sticks.

Jimmy wakes up. He realises it was all a dream and he was very sad. Jimmy gets dressed and goes through to the living room. There were three, new born bearded dragons waiting for him! He was very excited as had always wanted a pet!

THE EVIL SAND By Declan Cummings (P6)

6 am. New York City. "Lily, I'm heading out to work now "said Jeff heading out the door to the police station. "Ok," said Lily. "I'll see you for dinner, I'm cooking your favourite!"

"You're early" said Mark the chief inspector when Jeff arrived at work. "Yes I am" said Jeff. "Well Jeff, somebody has been murdered at the beach" said Mark angrily. "We need you to investigate now."

"But I'm...", Jeff was in the middle of explaining that he was allergic to sand before Mark cut him off.

"No buts!" barked Mark so Jeff sprinted to his car and drove to New Jersey beach, outside New York City. Jeff got out his car and saw his wife Lily lying there dead on the sand.

Jeff was heartbroken! Somebody had killed his wife! Jeff ran onto the sand before forgetting about his allergies. "Atchoo!" he sneezed. Jeff had to run off the beach before he got a red, nasty rash. What could he do? He went back to the station and asked Mark for help. They looked around Lily's body but there were no clues. Jeff and Mark took the body back to the lab. Mark had found a camera at the beach so Jeff checked the camera and saw a picture of himself killing Lily. When Mark asked who the man in the photograph was, Jeff didn't reply. Mark went through to the camera room and saw Jeff's photo.

"Jeff! You are under arrest for what you did! You killed Lilly!" shouted Mark.

"I didn't mean to! The sand made me do it!" exclaimed Jeff. "Its magic sand and every time I go near it, it makes me do strange things!"

Jeff was sent to prison. When he had served his time, he vowed he would never let the sand make him do something he didn't want to do again. He bought a house in the mountains, far away from the beach and spent the rest of his life climbing mountains.

THE HEADLESS CHICKEN BY LUKE FOXTON (P6)

Once upon a time, there was a headless chicken called Bobby. His family lived in Australia but he lived in Scotland. His family forgot to take him when they moved abroad and now it is his mission to get to Australia! His parents had given him £20,000 spending money which I'm sure you'll agree is very generous of them but there was one problem… THE FLIGHT SCHEDULE!!! As Bobby is a headless chicken, he cannot see, hear or smell but he can somehow still talk. So, he walked along to the airport and asked a passer-by, "Do you know where the flight to Australia is?" But the man that he asked was French and he said, "Bonjour Je m'appelle Jeff". So Bobby moved on.

He managed to find someone that was English but he ended up on the flight to Melbourne instead. "Oh no," Bobby exclaimed. "I wanted to get on the one to Sydney"! So when Bobby arrived in Melbourne, he had to spend another £100 to get the bus to Sydney. When he finally got to Sydney and arrived at his mum and dads house, they all lived happily ever after in their headless chicken house.

THE HOLE BY SINEAD BOYLE (P6)

Hi, my name is Jade. I'm 16 years old and I'm going to tell you a little bit about my story and what happened.

It was a long time ago. My best friend Aaron and I went with our class on a school trip to a camp site.

One day, the class found some caves near the camp site. Aaron and I stayed longer in the caves and Aaron locked me in a hole! After a few days, a rescue dog sniffed me out and a police man found me.

I went home and the police caught Aaron. He admitted to his crime. Aaron said he had locked me in the cave because I was popular and I was hanging around with other people and he had got jealous. Aaron got arrested and I was never troubled again.

THE INCIDENT OF MAY'S DIARY BY EVE MACLEOD (P6)

When May woke up in the morning, she noticed that her diary was missing. She woke up Emily, her big sister and said, "Why did you take my diary?"

Emily replied, "What are you talking about? I've been sleeping!"

May said "Nice try I'm not falling for that".

"What do you mean?", replied Emily.

"So…….you're saying you don't know what happened?"

Emily shouted "YES I HAVE NO IDEA!!"

"Okay then", said May.

Emily thought she could just go to sleep so she did.

"Emily wake up!", screamed May.

"What? I'm awake now! What is it? My friend Sarah is in the house, but how?" said Emily.

"Do you think she stole my diary?" said May.

"I don't know ask her", said Emily."

"Okay", said May.

May goes up to Sarah to say, "What are you doing in my house?"

Sarah said, "Um… sorry but I took your diary!"

May said "It's okay"

"Thanks for forgiving me!" said Sarah happily. She was sad that she had taken the diary.

"That's what friends are for!" May said.

Emily said, "Now I can go to sleep?"

May and Sarah say, "Yes, but can't you see your disturbing us?"

Emily says to herself, yes I am the disturbing one.

THE MONSTER MYSTERIES BY DECLAN MCLEAN (P6)

Josh opened his eyes he heard moaning from outside he looked out the window he shouted "mum" no answer. He ran down stairs nobody was there. He ran to his sister's room he found his sisters favourite teddy ripped on the floor. He opened the cupboard door he saw his dog. He got a fright. He went to find his dad he was a scientist maybe he knows what's going on. So he ran to his dad's office but while he was running he saw zombies. One looked like the postman. He thought to himself did everyone leave him behind or did they die? He kept running to his dads office and found his dad so Josh said "why is there zombies outside" so his dad replied "at the lab we tried to make a super human with a gem with powers" then the roof collapsed. It was the leader. So my dad shot him in the gem. The leader he was dead.

THE MYSTERY BY TAYLOR RAMSAY (P6)

Sarah was snuggled under a duvet and BANG!! Sarah heard a noise from the attic so she jumped out of her bed and she went upstairs to investigate, but the attic door was locked...so she hunted everywhere until she saw a shiny thing up on the shelf. Sarah said, "That must be the key!" But the shelf was too high up. Then she heard mum so she ran downstairs and went into her bed before her mum came in and gave her a row for being out of bed. After her mum went back to bed, she went back up to the attic with a chair and she put the chair down and stood on it. Sarah eventually managed to reach the key! She jumped back off the chair and put the key in the keyhole. She opened the door and the noise that had been terrifying Sarah all this time turned out to be her toy jack in the box!

THE PIRATE BY AARON DICKSON (P6)

Jon got up one day and looked out the window like he always did but this time he saw a big crowd of people. So he put on his clothes and ran outside. He went into the crowd to see what had happened and he saw a pirate ship! There was a mysterious map lying on the deck. He phoned his friend when they got to the ship Jon said you need to help me sneak on the ship his friend said fine but what for? I want to sail the sea said Jon. I always wanted to be a pirate.

So at midnight Jon and his friends sneaked past the people at the ship and jumped on the ship they got the map. Jon went up to the wheel and started to think he should look at the map and sail out to sea there was silence for a few minutes... they all said "let's go!" so Jon and his friends set out to sea. Let's look at the map, it is a treasure map we need to go find it said Jon. So we followed the map over the big waves then a massive sea monster appeared! It was green and yellow so we made lots of noise and it ran away. Finally the cave with the treasure we went in and got the treasure. And went home to our families.

THE TERRIFYING NIGHT AT FREDDY'S
BY MIA KUTLUOL (P6)

Emily's best friend Freddy had invited her round to his house for her birthday. She had just turned 11. Freddy had invited all her friends round and they had a great time. Later on, Emily went to the toilet. Out of the corner of her eye, she spotted a purple man. "What are you doing in the girl's toilet?" yelped Emily. There was no answer. The man grabbed Emily and ran away. "HELP"! Shouted Emily. There was a big scream. Bonnie, one of Emily's friends was in the next room and heard the commotion.

"Emily? Where are you?" yelled Bonnie.

"I'm in this room", screamed Emily. Bonnie ran to the room and opened the door and saw the purple man.

"I am the Purple man, do you want Emily?" asked Purple Man.

"Yes! Now hand her over please", said Bonnie.

"NEVER! HAHAHAHAH!" yelled purple man.

Bonnie grabbed Emily and ran away. "Thanks for saving me!" said Emily.

"You're welcome," said Bonnie.

Bonnie had saved the day.

THE UNFOUND MAZE BY KEVIN KERNACHAN (P6)

"Hi." My name is Nutty, I'm a peanut and I am 12 years old. The most mischievous maze in the world is in M&M land and I found this maze today by accident. When you get there, an interesting character will meet you at the entrance. He had the most amazing powers and his name was Mr Hazelnut. In the mischievous maze there were the scariest looking insects including spiders and bats everywhere.

As I entered the maze I heard a loud scream "Aaaaaaaaahhhhhhh!"

I recognised that scream. I'm sure it was Daisy, my best friend. I thought she'd gone on holiday!! Oh my goodness she must have been stuck in here all along!

"Daisy...Daisy! Is that you? Where are you? I can hear you but can't see you."

"I'm in the maze please save me now", shouted Daisy.

"I'm in the maze! I will try and find you, let me go and get Mr Hazelnut, he can help with his powers".

I ran to get Mr Hazelnut to help. After getting Mr Hazelnut we ran to get Daisy out. Mr Hazelnut used his power by firing peanut bombs the scary insects to freeze them on the spot.

"Don't move Daisy! We are just about there", I shouted.

"There you are! Aaaaaaahhhhhhhhh! I'm so happy to see you! I have been here for days", she said.

"Let's go home", I said.

Mr Hazelnut said, "We will have to roll slowly as the quicker you roll, the deeper the maze gets so don't roll too fast, ok. There's the gate jump on to me and I will get us out. Roll! Roll!

"We're out! WOO HOO we're safe", they all shouted.

THE ZOMBIE TAKEOVER BY DILLON HANNAH (P6)

"Jack we need to go!" said my Mum, "Why mum?" I said, "Zombies!" she shouted. "WHAT?!" I screamed. Then a zombie broke in through the window and grabbed my mum. The zombie ran for me, I dodged it and it went flying out a window. The zombie dropped a piece of paper out of his pocket. I picked it up and it said in small writing.

"The Z King's dog has a stone on its collar.
If you take it off everyone will be human again.
The dog is located at Buckingham Palace."

Great, that's close to my house. I ran and ran until I heard barking. I turned and there was the palace with a zombie dog in the gardens. I jumped over the gate and dodged past the zombie guards who tried to munch on my shoulder. The dog had the collar. I threw a stick and the dog picked it up and returned it. I quickly grabbed the collar off the dog and humans appeared everywhere. My mum ran and hugged me. Then there was silence. Next thing the Queen walked over she said "Jack, I'm giving you this medal for saving us and you can keep the dog". I said "Thanks so much Your Highness".

I called the dog Muncher. Sometimes when I look at Muncher, I think I see red eyes but I might just be imagining things...

ROBBY THE RABBIT BY BLAKE GIBSON (P6)

There was a rabbit called Robby. He and his Mum, Dad and sister were going on holiday to Australia and they were leaving the next day.

The next day they went to the seaside to find a boat and then they jumped on a boat and sailed away. When they got to Australia they went to a forest for the night. Robby woke up and no one could be found! There was a note at the tree…

It said we had to go back "hope you're ok" Robby said " how will I get home?" so he ran to the closed boat and jumped on the boat. 1 hour later he reached some rocks and the boat started to sink.

So Robby jumped on some jelly fish then a shark started to attack him. A dolphin came and saved Robby then took him home. When he got to France, he saw his sister she was crying he told her about his journey. It took her a while to realise it was her brother he saw his family they decided they are never going on holiday again

THE WEIRD CRISP PACKET BY THOMAS HUGHES (P6)

Once upon a time there *was* a boy called Bobby. He was a lonely kid. He lived in a little cottage in South England. One day he was getting ready for school and he was about to pick up his bag. He shouted "Mum I forgot my snack!" Mum replied "What would you like for break?" Bobby answered loudly "A packet of ready salted crisps please."

He set off for school. Once he got there he saw his friend Jake who asked him "Do you want a game of football?" Bobby said "Yeah let's go then" but the bell went for the start of school.

In English the class were planning stories and Jake wrote a note and threw it to Bobby. It said "meet me at lunch." The bell rang for lunch. Bobby went to see Jake but he couldn't find him. The next day he found out where he was. He had got sent home early

Then the next day he found the same crisp packet at his door that he had for his break. He was worried. On the way home, he heard a rustle behind him and he turned around "Oh it's only an old crisp packet". He walked a bit further on and he heard that rustle again. He picked it up and a rat jumped out!! Bobby got the fright of his life! He screeched "Aaaaah!!" And ran in his house

The following day the same crisp packet was at the end of his gate. He went and put it in the bin then he sprinted to school and just got there in time. Then he went home and the crisp packet wasn't there.

ZOE AND DRAGONS BY VICTORIA BLACHOWICZ (P6)

Zoe is 8 year girl and she has a pet dragon. Zoe loves dragons. But she still doesn't know where dragons live.

The next day, Zoe went to the park with her friend's Bob and Emma. She played some games. Zoe, Bob and Emma walked back home. Bob saw a big tree with doors. Bob, Emma and Zoe went in to the tree and then saw something fly!

It was a dragon.

Zoe looked around the tree and saw flying dragons everywhere. She was very happy.

Every week, Zoe went to the dragons and gave them food to eat. On their birthday Zoe gave dragon's birthday cake.

"Mum can we adopt these dragons? Said Zoe.

"No because we have a small house. Said mum.

"Ok" said Zoe.

"But you can go to the dragons house." Said mum.

"Ok" said Zoe.

Zoe was very happy about this.

On the next day Zoe went to see the dragons. The dragons were gone! Zoe cried but something stood next to Zoe. That was a blue dragon! Zoe jumped with joy and the blue dragon become her pet.

BELLA AND ASHLIE TRAPPED IN THE MUSEUM
BY ADAMA KRUBALLY (P7)

Once there were two girls called Bella and Ashlie who were best friends. They lived in Wisconsin. They loved art and going to the museum. They planned on going on a trip to Australia. On the day they were going to Australia they went to the museum one last time. They enjoyed looking at all the exhibits.

But when the tannoy was speaking they didn't hear that they had to leave. So when it was time for them to leave the door was locked. They totally freaked out so much they were about to explode.

Bella was looking around with Ashlie for something to escape with so they could catch their flight to Australia. Ashlie checked the time, it was 5:45 pm. They had been at the museum for 3 hours. But when Ashlie was typing something on her IPhone 5s She bumped into a window and it gave Bella an idea to look to see if all the windows were shut. Fortunately, one window was open so they climbed out. It was 6pm.

They hailed a taxi and just made it to the airport in time to catch their flight to Australia.

PARROTS JOURNEY By Brooke Clapperton (P7)

One warm day a parrot called Poppet who had lots of different colours and feathers was perching on a tall tree. Poppet lived in Brazil so it was very hot and very busy but one night Poppet had a very funny feeling that she had never had before. Suddenly Poppet had a little tingle in her foot. It was another parrot which was dark coloured and very angry. It said, "I am Jimmy," and it had lots more to say like, "Jimmy is very sad and angry because Jimmy has lost a good friend who went missing one day during a thunderstorm in the centre of Rio.

The next day Jimmy came back and asked, "Can you take me to Rio please?" Poppet agreed and told him to meet him by the tree that night.

That dark night in Brazil the two parrots started to fly to Rio. On the way there Poppet and Jimmy spotted a cool looking brazil nut which was on a big tree and had lots of nuts on it so they took a bunch each and ate them on the way to RiO.

They finally were in Rio but they still had to get to the centre of Rio. They waddled to the other side of the place they were in and had a little brazil nut that was solid and soggy but they ate it anyway because they were very thirsty and very sweaty.

Suddenly, they heard a noise coming from the centre of the fruit market. They went to investigate and they found Sam munching away at a peach and a melon and Sam was the double the size he was they last time Jimmy saw him. Sam told Jimmy that he got washed away by the storm and ended up in amongst the fruit stalls and has been munching food ever since .

CLOVER McHEN AND THE CURIOUS INCIDENT OF THE MISSING FRIEND BY ELLIE LOGAN (P7)

My best friend was gone. Scratches on all of the barn walls. By the way, I'm a chicken, fifteen cm tall. I have coppery feathers. I live on a farm outside of Edinburgh. I love mysteries. I have a picture of Sherlock Holmes on one of the walls of my chicken coop. I hoped I would be able to find my friend. And soon.

It was a rainy day when Gabby the goose went missing. She was Canadian. When I walked into the barn I found the walls covered in deep scratches, feathers in a pile and Gabby's favourite purple scarf in a crumpled pile. This needed detective work.

While I walked outside the barn looking for clues, I saw fat, chunky paw prints. Badger paw prints. I ran to the farmer's house yelling, "Snuff, I know who kidnapped Gabby!"

The old, brown and black sniffer dog woke from a midday nap. "Who was it?" Snuff asked. I explained that wild animals took her.

We followed the paw prints at sunset. An albino fox, a big, bulky badger and an evil seagull surrounded us. I scratched the seagull with my right talons. Snuff growled at the other two and scared them off.

We ran, ran faster than we ever did. The paw prints led us to an old, brown, decaying building. There was a window outside. When we looked in we saw Gabby in a cage, another albino fox guarding her.

I saw a stone on the ground. I threw it in a hole in the building. Snuff and I ran in. I used one of my talons to pick the lock. "We're here to rescue you," I clucked. Success! The cage door opened. We ran out of the building, down a path, through a few back gardens, and made it back before sunrise. We let Gabby lie down in her nest and rest

We were all safe and sound.

When Gabby woke up at noon, I told her what we did to rescue her.

Me, Snuff and gabby went to the barn. Gabby lifted out a bright red box with gold corners. Gabby lifted out two lilac scarves. One for me, and one for snuff. "For acts of heroism, above the line of duty," Gabby explained, "For being my… friends!"

The young goose was almost in tears, with joy. I also shed a few tears. I also thought I saw Snuff wipe one away with a paw

That's my curious incident. What's yours?

CURIOUS DOG OF THE NIGHT TIME
BY FRANK LOW (P7)

Once upon a time there was a deadly dog who got up to evil deeds!

One Dark, foggy night in the middle of winter, Sammy, the dog, went to his secret hut at the bottom of the garden to hatch a plot.

He decided to start a dog war so he could be the ruler of all dogs!

The next day he went round stealing all the other dogs' dinners then told them that it was the gang of dogs from the opposite side of the river.

They all charged over the bridge, looking for a fight! The other dogs managed to persuade them that it hadn't been them as they had all been at a dog reunion.

They knew that someone was telling porky pies. All evidence led to the other dogs' gang hut. They headed there and discovered all their dinners lying in a pot. Sammy was the culprit!

They waited till he returned then asked him if he was responsible. He had to admit it because the evidence was right there in front of his own eyes!

As a punishment they made Sammy eat all of the food he had stolen until he was feeling very sick!

"Baaarf!"

DEFUSE MISSION BY ELLIOT DEVRIES (P7)

One day in Iraq in a jelly factory there was a terrorist attack. Their plan was to plant a C4 Explosive and a counter terrorism force found out and they had an hour to defuse the bomb...

The counter terrorism force set out and found the jelly factory but the terrorists had guns and weren't afraid to shoot.

Luckily they had guns in the back of their trunk. 30 minutes left!

The counter terrorists charged in but no one was there. Only twenty minutes left! So they looked for the bomb. 1 of the terrorists was spotted and arrested. With ten seconds left they found it. 5,4,3,2,1. They had defused it on the last second so they lived to tell the story and the rest of the terrorists were sent to a death sentence or a life in prison.

FRIENDSHIP BY SEAN MCCORMACK (P7)

One day Harry and Simon were talking when Simon said, "Can I get £100 because I have no money"?

Harry said, "Ok, but pay me the money when you get it."

"Thanks," Simon said.

Two weeks later Harry said, "Do you have the money yet?"

"I'm not giving it back!"

"THEN GET OUT!" so Simon left.

So Harry tried to think of how to make money quickly so he joined a football club but Simon was in the same team so they were thrown together every week and started to become pals again. Simon paid the money back and now they are best friends!

THE MURDER... BY LANA WILSON (P7)

The body was found on top off a rock at the beach. It was drenched in water and covered in sand. I heard a policeman say that it looked like it had been washed up on the shore. I tried to get a closer look but the policeman would not let me though there was a slight crack in between. I peered through and I could make out the slight figure of the body but I could not tell the identity. It looked like he or she could have been thirteen or fourteen. I wasn't sure. I only got a quick look. After that I left because it was getting too crowded. That night I was woken up by a loud thump by my door. The policeman came in and arrested me. I asked why and he said I was being arrested for murder. When I got down to the station they gave me new clothes and they took my belongings. The next again day I overheard a policeman say I was going to be prosecuted.

THE HATCH IN THE PARK BY JACK BROWN (P7)

"Mum, Clark and I are going to the park," said Sam."

"Ok," said Sam's mum shouting down the stairs.

When they got to the park they almost got in a fight with four boys but Clark had managed to talk them out of the fight. He said he would give them all of his dinner money and Sam agreed with the idea. He agreed with that idea because if he didn't he would have got bullied. After the boys had been on the roundabout they went on the swings. They were having so much fun until Sam fell off the swing. When he fell he felt something wooden underneath him so the boys swept away the bark. After they had finished sweeping away the bark they found a hatch. They opened the hatch and went down into it. They found a house hidden underground and they started exploring. They both went into different rooms.

In the room in the middle they heard a weird sound. They both thought it was each other but it wasn't any of them so they entered the room but there wasn't anything there. They looked at each other. When they looked back there was a weird man standing in front of them. He was wearing a suit and he had the palest face the boys had ever seen. The boys were more scared than they had ever been before so they ran away and alerted the police. The park got closed down as it was now an investigation. When the boys got to the police station they got questioned about the incident. They told the police everything they had seen and waited to see what would happen?

EMILY'S PET BUNNY BY LUCY McDONALD (P7)

Emily woke up one morning and she raced down stairs because she knew that her mum had a surprise. When she got down stairs her mum handed her a box so she opened the box and it was a bunny.

So later that day she invited her best friend over. Emily showed her friend her bunny.

They played with her bunny all day and they all named it together .They decided to call it Tiger because it was a boy.

The next morning they went down in to the living room and the bunny was gone. It was gone for good. She decided to go on a big hunt.

She called all her friends and she told them the bad news.

They hunted and hunted but they could not find him. 30 minutes had already passed. Still no sign!

5 minutes later, they found Tiger lying dead and motionless on the path.

They lifted him up and carried him back home.

Her mum was at the door.

What should she tell her??????????

RAB & MACARONI BY KAI DALGLEISH (P7)

Rab sees a weird shadow. Rab is a blob and Macaroni is an alien who wants to be friends.

Rab's challenge is to overcome his fear with the shadow. Rab asked Macaroni to go in for a cup of tea. Macaroni said "Tea makes my spaceship work. " Rab and Macaroni go to Macaroni land where they crashed the spaceship and aliens were everywhere. Rab moves there for ever. Rab and his alien friends go on an adventure to Storm Island ...

RECORD By Ben Wanless (P7)

One day a twelve year old boy called Harry woke up. In the morning and put on his favourite hoodie which was blue. He was going to his favourite cake shop, Lee Bears Cakes. He was going there because Lee Bears wanted to tell him something. Lee told him that he was making the biggest cake in history! Harry told Lee that he was raising money to parachute off the moon! Lee said he would try and help. They set up a fund raiser. Harry ran from the café to the castle at the top off the hill and Lee sold some cakes. They raised one million pounds! They went halvers, 500k each. Lee started making his cake and Harry was in his rocket ship about to take off!

10,9,8,7,6,5,4,3,2,1, Blast off!

He was off.

An hour later he arrived at the moon. He was ready to jump. He did, and he was falling faster that light. He was in earth's orbit! He was 500ft. he pulled on his parachute and he drifted down. Lee had just finished making his cake then "Bang!" Harry landed on the cake. He was sorry but he had just broken the world record but it was the record for the highest parachutist into the biggest cake! They were so happy and they had a party to celebrate.

THE INVISIBLE MAN BY REECE LOTHIAN (P7)

One day the invisible man called Reece was walking in the garden when he discovered an enormous footprint. Who could it belong to? He had no idea! He needed to find out who the mysterious creature was.

Reece decided to see if the monster would come back so he went behind a big tree and he fell asleep. When he woke up he was no longer invisible.

He had clicked his fingers and he discovered what broke the spell.

WHO DO THEY BELONG TO?

BY SHAHED METGAWIL (P7)

Kacey and Rocky were standing next to the fountain in the middle of the city. They found a magnifying glass and an alien mask in the fountain. They worked so hard to discover who they belonged to. They looked for clues and asked people if they belonged to them. After a few hours they found an alien who has been left behind by his space ship.

The alien was green and small with one eye. The alien told them he was from Mars. He told them that he wants to find his way home. They found out that the magnifying glass and the alien mask belong to him.

SHEPHERD IN THE NIGHT BY CALUM TAIT (P7)

One night Rob the shepherd woke up at 3.25am on a Friday morning. He found his lights turning on and off. He saw shadows all around him, he got really freaked out. He went down stairs to get breakfast and found his Rice Krispies and his bread scattered all over the floor.

He knew something was wrong, he had never heard of this in his life. He thought he had a ghost in his house but he didn't believe in them. So there couldn't be. He went back up to his room with nothing to eat so he was narky. He fell asleep and was woken up by the same thing but this time he heard whistling down stairs and heard music but he couldn't understand what music it was. He knew it was old music but didn't know what band it was. So he went down the stairs and saw a floating plate hovering above everything.

Then there was a ghost sitting whistling on a bunker top with a mean look on his face...

SPARTAN AND THE MAGIC KEY
BY MARCIN STRZESZNIEWSKI (P7)

Once upon a time Spartan read a book and found a magical key. This key opened a special book which was about planet Mars. Spartan wanted wings but his family was poor. Spartan's dad had a rocket so his dad gave the rocket to Spartan. Now Spartan was able to fly to Mars in the rocket ship. Spartan was on Mars he found a magical book. He put the key in the book, the magical book opens and has a light so you can read it. Spartan stayed there for one whole week without his family. Finally he went home in his dad's rocket ship and he said, "Thank you dad."

He brought the magical book and key back home and magical things began to happen............

THE ATTACK BY JACK ANDERSON (P7)

One day there was an Attack by terrorists and two boys tried to stop it.

Those boy's names were Rob Weller and Vin Petrol and they heard it on the news.

Then they set off into action. They went to the terrorists' territory and it was illuminated by neon lights, guards everywhere and was in a secret ice cream factory called Chuckleway.

It was a bomb attack. They set a bomb in an ice cream tub and there were more than 1000 tubs so they had to do it quickly or "BOOM!" the whole factory would be blown up with ice cream.

The boys went through the door and looked through tubs. "Aha found it," said Rob. Then Vin said, "Quick, I hear guards." Then a guard shouted, "Get out before I call the cops!" Two minutes left, so he looked at the bomb again.

Fifty seconds left. "WHAT COLOUR IS IT?"

Beep, beep, beep, beep, beep, beep. BOOM! ICE CREAM EVERYWHERE!!!!!

THE BIG FIGHT!!! BY CLOE LYONS (P7)

Amelia and Kate are best friends. Until Amelia gets a boyfriend. His name is Lucas and Kate fancies him. But she doesn't want to split them up. But her feelings are getting stronger for Lucas. Then one day Kate is talking to Lucas at school and comes out with it "I love you," Lucas didn't know what to say. Then Amelia comes.

One day Kate feels like she should tell Amelia that she has feelings for Lucas. Kate told Amelia and she went crazy. And after that they never spoke again.

Kate keeps trying to split Amelia and Lucas up for 4 months. But it didn't work Amelia went up to Kate and said "STOP TRYING TO SPLIT US UP OR ELSE!" Then walked away. Kate went to Amelia's house because she was sick of not talking to Amelia. When Amelia opened the door she slapped Kate in the face. They started fighting they fought for 10 more minutes.

Kate ran away after that night. No one saw her for weeks no one knew where she was or heard from her. Amelia felt so bad and blamed herself for Kate running away! She went looking for Kate and found her at a bus stop! She ran up to her and gave her a hug. "This is all my fault!" said Amelia. How about none of us go out with Lucas. Just come home please. "OK".

THE MISSING CAT BY ANGEL PRESTON (P7)

There were two boys, their names were Liam and Lee. They were going to the park to play on the swings. They were thinking about Mrs Floss's cat that ran away last night. It   was awkward because Lee wasn't talking or mucking around. He was quiet for a change. Liam told Lee not to be upset about the Cat. "Lee don't be upset about her cat it will be fine," in a low voice.

I..I....I really don't know what to say about it as I am really scared, in a sad voice.

"We will go home, get changed and we will have a hunt for the cat."

"Yes we will look for the Cat," in an amazed voice.

As they were walking home they went into the forest and as they were walking they saw a little ginger fluffy cat sitting on the cold, wet, muddy, rough ground. The boys were so proud that they found Star in the forest. They went over to pick her up and she looked so lonely. Lee picked her up and petted her and took her to Mrs Floss's house. She opened her door with a surprised look on her face.

"OHH THANK YOU BOYS THANK YOU SO MUCH!" in an excited voice.

"We'll we need to go for our dinner so I will speak to you later."

As the boys were crossing over the road they stopped and gave each other a high five and said good job. The boys went into Lees and have fish and chips with apple juice.

"I am so proud of what we did today and I hope my mum and dad will be as well and your mum and dad. As they were speaking their parents came in and said,

"We heard that you found Mrs Floss's cat." "WELL DONE!"" in a happy, clear voice.

THE SQUIRREL AND THE COFFEE BEAN PATCH
BY LEWIS HUNTER (P7)

One day a squirrel went to a coffee patch and asked for some coffee and took it back to his habitat.

There was also a random man who went to the exact same place to have coffee with his friends.

By the next day, the squirrels had had too much coffee so they decided to take over the world.

The random guy is the only person left who can save the world so he made friends with the coffee plantation owner.

He found out from the owner what kind of thing would destroy the coffee plants.

Next, he hired a helicopter and flew over the coffee plants and sprayed them with poison. The plants all died and the squirrel reverted back to normal and the world was saved.

THE HELMET BY JASON BATEMAN (P7)

Buzz Lightyear's helmet was gone. He looked everywhere but there was no helmet. He had to find a way to open the window. He climbed on the toy box. Woody said, "What are you doing?"

"My helmet is gone we have to find it."

"To the ship."

"BLAST OFF!" "No mistakes so far."

"Oh no, asteroids we're doomed!" "Snap out of it, it's over," I said.

"I should have known evil Emperor Zirg would have had my helmet."

I dived in and Woody went after me. He shut the door. There was a lever on the wall so I jumped on Woody's shoulders and pulled the lever and the door opened. I grabbed my helmet but the computer said self-destruct in 5 seconds. We ran to the ship. 3,2,1,0. We were gone.

Zirg was gone forever or was he?...

THE KILLER BY KAL BRECHIN (P7)

BREAD

One dark and stormy night a spaceship crash landed in a field.

The police had arrived at the scene. They inspected the ship but they couldn't find anything so they got back in their car. But, little did they know, a dangerous slice of bread was on board whose main goal was to destroy the world starting with the police.

So the bread climbed onto the roof of the police car and dropped onto the driver's seat and the car crashed.

BUT, THIS WAS JUST THE BEGINNING!!!!!!

THE MURDER... BY LANA WILSON (P7)

The body was found on top off a rock at the beach. It was drenched in water and covered in sand. It looked like it washed up at shore. I heard a policeman say. I tried to get a closer look but the policeman would not let me though there was a slight crack in between. I peered through and I could make out the slight figure of the body but I could not tell the identity. It looked like he or she could have been thirteen or fourteen. I wasn't sure. I only got a quick look. After that I left because it was getting too crowded. That night I was woken up by a loud thump by my door. The policeman came in and arrested me. I asked why and he said I was being arrested for murder. When I got down to the station they gave me new clothes and they took my belongings. The next again day I overheard a policeman say I was going to be prosecuted.

MYSTERIOUS INCIDENT OF THE MISSING PARENTS
BY REBECCA WILLIAMSON (P7)

Emily woke with nothing but the sound off birds chirping. She flung her covers and stood up. The floor was cold almost as if she was walking on water. She started walking to Eduardo's room.

But he was not there. Emily then walked out of Eduardo's room and down stairs. She stood at the foot off the kitchen door. No one was there but there was a mysterious mess made up of toast crumbs, Coco pops and the kettle had steam coming out of it but it stopped after a while.

Then in came Eduardo. "Have you by any chance seen mum and dad?" asked Eduardo "No why?" said Emily confused. "They're gone!" "They're not anywhere. I have been everywhere but I can't find them!"

After trying to call their cell phone and looking everywhere they decided to look for them. Patrick and Sarah Mikal.

After two years of trying to find them we found a woman called Mrs. Grounder was willing to take Emily and Eduardo in on the condition that they forget about their parents and stop trying to find them.

One day Emily and Eduardo were sitting with Mrs. Grounder in the sitting room when they heard the doorbell ring. "Hello," said Mrs. Grounder.

"Hello, we are Sarah and Patrick Mikal…"

THE RIFT BY GEORGIA GARDINER (P7)

Mike has been gone for six months. No-one knows what happened, or if he's even alive. My name is Sophie Jones. I am fifteen years old. Mike was my best friend but he's gone now. As I walk to school I discover a strange glowing orb. It begged for me to walk towards it, I touched it. Suddenly I end up in a place that looked like space. I like space. I walk around. I see someone, he looks familiar. Mike? It's Mike! I run towards him, he stands there staring. "Mike!" He won't answer. "Mike what's wrong?" "You left me," he says "you left me for all this time," I tell him "Then we'll leave," he speaks again "NO! I will never go with you!" I try to leave but he grabs me and pushes me to the ground. He hurts me over and over again. I can't hurt him, he was a friend. Or was he? He hurts me even more. I attack. We end up fighting, throwing and blocking punches. Then I see an amulet. It gives him power. It helps him survive. I rip it off and beat him to the ground. He stops fighting back, he stops moving. He stops breathing. The amulet glows in my hand, it glows so bright I shield my eyes. I end up back home and the orb is gone. And so is Mike. It has been two years and I have regretted what I've done since that day. Mike is gone forever, and it was all my fault.

THE SHOPPING SPREE By Caitlin Brechin (P7)

Mum, Willie, KAL and I went on a shopping spree, We tried to get as much food as possible. Then we suddenly found ourselves in a maze. We were stuck and couldn't get out. A giant monster appeared. Mum was protecting me. Next, Willie's eyes went red. "No," I said. I turned round and mum and KAL had also turned evil. Then the whole world turned evil, even the royal family including Prince George!

THE WITHER BY JACK MACLEOD (P7)

Somewhere in the Minecraft world lived a lonely Miner called Lauchlan.
Lauchlan mined and mined all day long so he could make tools. One Day while he
was mining he saw a man stuck in the cave. He said, "Are you ok?
The man said, "Yes, but can you help me?" Lauclan said,
"Yes." Lauclan asked,
"Whats your name?" he said.
"My name is Preston," he said.
"I am a lava mob, do you want to be friends?" Preston said,
"Yes," so they went to Preston's house and Lauclan moved all his stuff over.
They made Armour, pick axes and shovels to do some work around the house,
kill Zombies, Creepers and some Skeletons.
One day they went to fight the Wither and they saw four people all together
looking at them.
Lauclan shouted, "Hello."
They shouted, "Hello," back,
"What are your names?" they said.
"Rob," "Vikkstar123," and "Mitch," and "Jerome," so they teamed up.
"Do use want to fight the Wither?" They said,
"Yes," "let's work together. We have got 20000 Golden apple."
"Nice," "Can we have some?"
"Yes," they said.
"Ok, let's do this."
So they fought and fought and fought till The Wither was dead.